Cooper and Me™
and the Military

Written by Monique & Alexa Peters

Illustrated by Alexa Peters & Melissa Peterson

Education Advisory Committee
Our advisors review each book in the *Cooper and Me* series
and have earned degrees from these universities, among others:
Ann Beasley, B.S. from St. John's University
Karen Lunny, M.A. from George Mason University
Carolyn Olivier, M.Ed. from Harvard Graduate School of Education

To order additional copies of this book or other books in this series:
www.CooperandMe.com

Cooper and Me books
are proudly printed in the
U.S.A.

This book is dedicated to all the wonderful families who serve our country, especially Tami, Gracie, and Mark Hilton, who inspired us to write this special addition to our series.

Cooper and Me thanks Nathaniel Ledwith for his literary expertise.

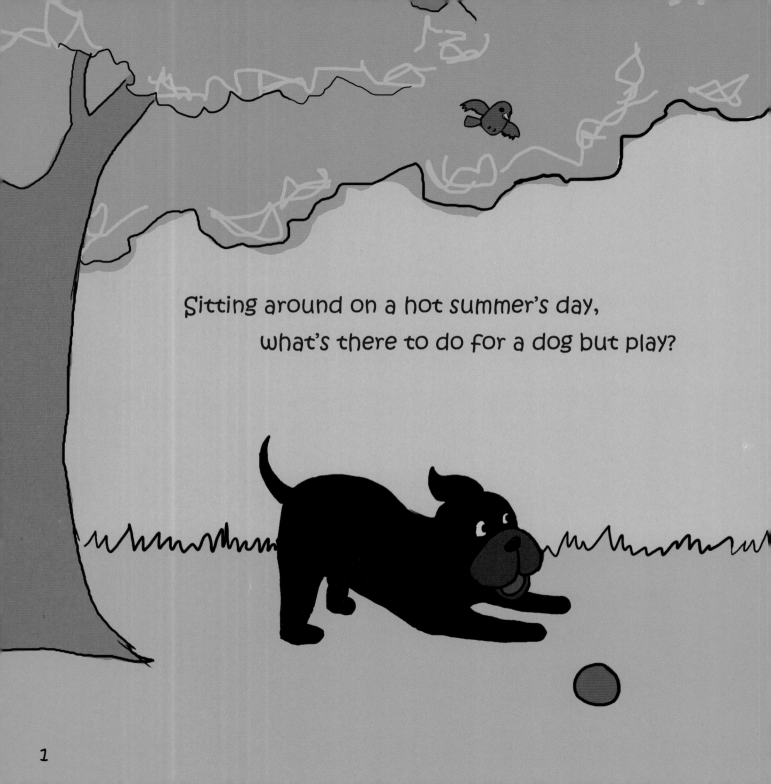

Sitting around on a hot summer's day,
what's there to do for a dog but play?

1

"Cooper, quick!
Before it gets dark,
get your ball,
and let's go to the park!"

2

So out we went, with a leash round his neck,
ready to make the most of our trek.

We walked out the door,
ran down the street,

and when we got to the park,
who did we meet?

He was a neighborhood dog from around the bend.
His name was Trooper. It was Cooper's best friend!

He was there with my friends, Gracie and Joe,
two of the nicest kids you could know.

Their mom and their dad were both far away,
serving our country day after day.

7

There they'd met Trooper, who served every day,

and watched after soldiers
in bed where they lay.

8

He was very well trained
to serve and to save.

People were grateful
for all that he gave.

9

Then one day, while making their rounds,
the troops heard Trooper making sad sounds.

His leg was hurt,
    though he tried his best.
        He obviously needed a vet and some rest.

My friends' parents knew what to do.
They'd give Trooper a home
and their kids a dog, too!

They came home with Trooper for Gracie and Joe,
but soon again back to work they'd both go.

One day I said, "We should write them a letter!

Send them some pictures!

I'm sure you'll feel better!"

15

So we wrote up the letters, took pictures galore,

but Joe said he wanted to do something more.

He left and came back with a little stuffed pup.

"When I'm feeling down,

Trooper makes me feel up!"

"This pup will be from me and from you,
so Mom and Dad can have
a Trooper there, too!"

We taped up the box, and once it was sealed,
dropped it off at the post office down by the field.

It traveled over countries, over rivers and seas,
to land at the base where their parents would be.

20

MAIL

When they arrived back,
   the package was there,

  with both of their names
     written slowly with care.

MOM AND DAD

They opened it up, and both looked inside.
They saw letters and pictures, then their eyes opened wide.

It was Trooper, their pup,

from their kids, whom they love,

delivered by train and by plane from above.

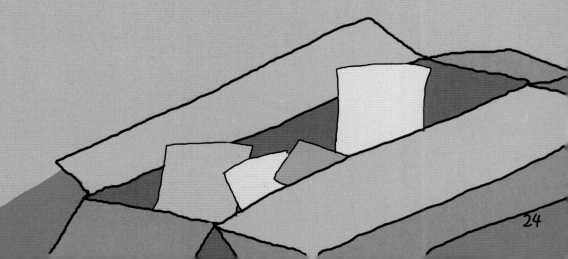

The End!

My Letter

Dear Service Men and Women,

My name is _____, and I wanted to thank you
for helping our country and keeping us safe. I am _____ years old, and I live
in the state of _____. I like to play _____
_____.

What do you like to do? I just wanted you to know how much I appreciate you.

Sincerely,

_____

To send letters and messages to our troops, check out this website:
www.ourmilitary.mil/letter-and-messages

Life Lesson
Staying Connected With Loved Ones
Even When You Can't Be Together

Sometimes loved ones have to spend many days away. For some families, they spend months apart. It's important for family members to stay connected when they spend so much time away from each other. Today, families can communicate in many ways with each other when they can't be together. Some of these ways include by phone, computer, Skype, videos, or sending cards, letters, or packages. The most important thing is to always remember that even when our loved ones aren't with us, they still love us and think of us. It's creating memories and sharing events that keep us close.

Connections

🐾 Have you ever missed someone? How does that feel?

🐾 What are some things you can do to feel closer to people you love who are far away?

🐾 What is your favorite memory with someone who doesn't live close to you?

Cooper and Me
and the
Military

Learning Together

🐾 **Where do the little girl and Cooper go?**
The little girl and Cooper go to the park.

🐾 **When they go to the park, who do they meet?**
The meet Trooper, Cooper's friend, at the park.

🐾 **Who are the little girl's friends?**
The little girl's friends are Gracie and Joe.

🐾 **What do Gracie and Joe's mom and dad do?**
Gracie and Joe's mom and dad serve our country in the armed forces. They work to protect us and keep us safe.

🐾 **Does Trooper serve his country, too?**
Yes, Trooper serves the U.S.A., too. U.S.A. stands for United States of America. He watches over soldiers while they sleep, and he is trained to serve and save people.

🐾 **When Trooper gets hurt, what does he need to do to get better?**
When Trooper gets hurt, he needs to see a vet. A vet is short for a veterinarian, and they are doctors for animals. A vet is also short for veteran. Veterans are people who have served our country. Maybe his vet was a vet!

🐾 **Where does Trooper go and who takes him there?**
Gracie and Joe's parents bring Trooper back to their home so that their kids can have a dog, and they can take care of him.

🐾 **Why are Gracie and Joe sad?**
Gracie and Joe are sad because their mom and dad have to leave again and go back to work.

Learning Together

🐾 **Have you ever felt sad when someone you love has to leave?**
Open discussion.

🐾 **What do Gracie and Joe do to feel better when their mom and dad leave?**
Gracie and Joe decide to write their parents a letter and send them some pictures to make them feel better.

🐾 **What do you think you can do if you miss your parents or loved ones?**
Open discussion. Talk about sharing memories or special events. Letting loved ones know what you've been doing or what you will be doing while they are away can keep them close at heart.

🐾 **What does Joe want to send to his mom and dad?**
Joe wants to send his mom and dad a stuffed toy puppy that looks like Trooper.

🐾 **Where do they go to send their package?**
They go to the post office down by the field. A post office is a place that delivers and receives letters and packages.

🐾 **Have you ever mailed any packages or letters to your loved ones?**
Open discussion.

🐾 **Have you ever received a package in the mail, and how did it make you feel?**
Open discussion. Talk about emotions like happy, sad, or excited, and why you felt that way.